Abdul

Butterfly

Collins
R E D
Storybook

Other Red Storybooks for you to enjoy:

King Rat *Bernard Ashley*
The Puppy Present *Jean Ure*
Whistling Jack *Linda Newbery*
The Dream Snatcher *Kara May*
The Witch's Tears *Jenny Nimmo*
Spider McDrew *Alan Durant*
Sasha and the Wolfcub *Ann Jungman*

Abdullah's Butterfly

JANINE M. FRASER

ILLUSTRATED BY
KIM GAMBLE

Collins
An imprint of HarperCollins*Publishers*

For Trevor, with love - J.M.F
For Anne - K.G.

First published in Australia by HarperCollins*Publishers* Pty Ltd in 1996
First published in Great Britain by Collins in 1998
Collins is an imprint of HarperCollins*Publishers* Ltd
77-85 Fulham Palace Road, Hammersmith, London, W6 8JB

1 3 5 7 9 8 6 4 2

Text copyright © Janine M. Fraser 1996
Illustrations copyright © Kim Gamble 1996

ISBN 0 00 675385 X

The author and illustrator assert the moral right to be identified
as the author and illustrator of the work.

Printed and bound in Great Britain by Caledonian International
Book Manufacturing Ltd, Glasgow G64

Chapter One

Magic moments fly willy-nilly out of
nowhere, as marvellously and unexpectedly
as a jewel-winged butterfly landing on your
shoulder. At least, that is how it seems to me.
Because just such a magic moment came and
brought with it a story, this story. And in the
pages of this book, the moment is kept like
a bright, pressed flower, forever magic.

The very first time I saw Abdullah (before
I even knew that Abdullah was his name),
I passed him on the mountain road running,
running with his outstretched arm clutching
a long-handled net. Running and running
up the mountain after the largest, brightest
butterfly I had ever seen.

A coating of dust gave him a pair of light brown socks on his bare, dark feet, and his hair was slicked black and unruly against his forehead, wet with sweat.

I passed him slowly thinking what a
pretty sight they made, Malaysian boy
and large, green butterfly, and I wished
I could stop to take a photo. But the road
was winding and narrow, and there was
no place to stop safely.

And so I just waved and smiled and
drove on. On and on, up to the village
of the family of my Malaysian friend,
to visit and leave them the parcels and
letters from her, as I had promised.

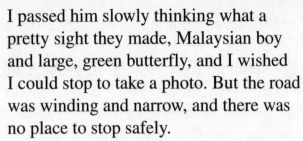

I didn't know then that it was Abdullah's village, too, perched high on the edge of the mountain where the forest grows thick and tall. I was just a visitor, a tourist who knew nothing of life in this country, nothing of the hardness of life in a Malaysian mountain village.

That is my excuse.

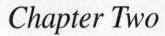

Chapter Two

Halfway up the mountain, I stopped the car where a waterfall tumbled down and skittered under a bridge. On the other side of the road and down a little, there was a market stall spilling its wares along the roadside. I got out and stretched and admired the forest view.

I walked over to the stall. Hand-moulded terracotta pots of every size were stacked high and higgledy-piggledy. Large bamboo mats were rolled tight and leant drunkenly against the wooden walls, and bamboo-woven purses and bags hung from jutting nails. Souvenirs too numerous to mention lay in untidy heaps on a rough bench alongside bananas and yams, papaya, small sweet pineapples and bunches of green vegetable.

Amongst it all lay three small, bright-hued butterflies framed with outspread wings, labelled and pinned to white board under glass.

'Oh no,' I breathed. 'How cruel.'

A woman wrapped in a faded sarong and tatty T-shirt came forward from the depths of the stall.

'You want to buy, yes?' she asked. 'Beautiful butterfly, only ten ringgit.'

I shook my head.

'Eight ringgit,' she insisted. 'Just for you, eight ringgit.'

But I shook my head, and moved away.

'Seven ringgit,' she called.

No. Butterflies were meant to be flying free, not pinned and framed and sold to be hung on a wall. I walked indignantly back towards the car.

Hearing a shout, I stopped and looked around. Running, running with his net outstretched, was the boy I had passed earlier on the road. He looked even more dusty and hot than before, and still the brilliant, green butterfly fluttered on ahead.

And that is when time stopped suddenly
still, in this magic of magical moments,
when the butterfly fluttered over and
settled gently on my shoulder.

I held my breath to hold the moment,
scared to breathe in case I frightened
it away.

I watched it lift and lower its black and emerald wings, revealing sapphire stripes beneath, and the rich ruby pattern on its black velvet belly. I watched its long black antennae flex and tremble.

So transfixed was I that for a moment I forgot where I was, forgot the boy.

Until he spoke. 'Don't move,' he said, stalking, intent with his net. 'Don't move.'

I didn't know Abdullah then, the hardness of his life, the struggle just to live from day to day. Not then.

And that is my excuse.

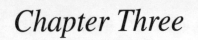

Chapter Three

Now it is time for Abdullah's story, as he told it to me.

His story begins in a little house on stilts, in a village on a mountain covered thick with rainforest in the highlands of Malaysia. This is where Abdullah lives.

The walls of his house are woven bamboo
and the roof of thatched palm from the
forest. Sometimes the rain drips through
onto the bamboo mats and into the carved
wooden bowls that Abdullah's mother puts
down. Sometimes the small, bold forest
monkeys come in through the window to
steal papaya and banana, and sometimes
Abdullah shares his sleeping mat with mice
and beetles.

But always, almost every day it seems to him, it is Abdullah's job to cut the forest back, to keep the vines and ferns and bamboo from taking over everything. Left to itself it would choke their tiny vegetable plantation and banana and papaya trees.

Sometimes Abdullah dreams in the night that it grows so thick and fast it traps them in the house and in their beds. He wakes up moaning and squalling and his mother comes running to see if he has been bitten by a spider or a scorpion.

But it is only a dream, thank goodness.

Abdullah lives with his mother and his grandfather on the outside forest edge of the village. For as long as he can remember, it has always been just his mother and Grandfather, and himself of course. When Abdullah was very small he rode high on Grandfather's shoulders, and as he grew Grandfather taught him everything he knew.

How to plant pineapple and tend it to ripeness; how to climb the tallest coconut palms and knock down the ripest coconuts; and how to carve the wooden eating bowls.

He taught Abdullah the best way to thatch the roof of their house to keep out the monsoon torrents, and he taught Abdullah to weave bamboo almost as well as himself.

Because once, Grandfather was
the best bamboo weaver in the village.

It was Grandfather who wove the thick
weaving for the walls of the houses.
It was Grandfather who wove the most
intricately-patterned sleeping mats, and
mats for the floors.

It was Grandfather who wove the
prettiest and sturdiest of baskets, for
taking the produce down to market.

And it was Grandfather who wove
the finest, lightest weaving, from the
finest, thinnest threads of bamboo, for
Abdullah's butterfly net.

Abdullah's butterfly net is his most treasured possession. Everywhere Abdullah goes, his net goes with him.

Brandishing its long bamboo handle and whisking the gossamer-thin net through the air, he captures countless jungle creatures. Beetles and dragonflies and scorpions and green forest frogs.

But it is the jewel-winged butterflies, the most elusive and wonderful of all forest creatures, that Abdullah wants most in his net.

Chapter Four

Each day, Abdullah's mother and
Grandfather walk down into the village to
the weaving workshop. There, Abdullah's
mother sits on her weaving mat, weaving
basket bottom after basket bottom, ready
for the weaver sitting beside her to take
up and weave the sides.

  Now it is Grandfather's job to pull
spliced bamboo through the vice to make
long, thin strips suitable for weaving.
Hundreds of long, thin strips, every day.
Because now, Grandfather's hands are
too stiff and his eyes too old for him to
be the best weaver in the village.

Most days after morning school, hoping
to earn one sen or two, Abdullah goes
to the weaving workshop and sweeps up
all the bamboo shavings and stacks the
bamboo strips in neat and tidy piles.
Sometimes, he is allowed to weave up
the basket sides like Grandfather has
shown him. Abdullah thinks that one day
he would like to be the best weaver in
the village, just like Grandfather.

And so, they earn a little money to live.
Not much. Never enough. Never enough
for new shoes for Abdullah, or a bright new
sarong for his mother. And sometimes, not
often enough, there is just enough money
to buy from Mr Chee's shop the porridge
that Grandfather likes so much, because his
teeth are all gone.

Chapter Five

Every daybreak, Abdullah is woken
by the raucous shrieks of forest parrots,
and the morning bickering and chatter
of forest monkeys.

He rolls up his sleeping mat and stows
it in a corner, and quickly pulls on shorts
and shirt for school. Abdullah's school
starts early in the morning and finishes
early after lunch. He is always in a rush
to catch the bright yellow school bus that
bumps and shudders down the road to
the big town school at the bottom of the
mountain.

Each day, as Abdullah sets off for school
he shrugs into the straps of his satchel and
snatches up his butterfly net from beside
the door. His mother puts in papaya and
banana and flat pancakes for his lunch.
She smooths his hair and tells him to study
hard and listen to the teacher, because she
wants him to do better than weave baskets
and catch butterflies for the rest of his life.

But Grandfather reaches for his hand as he
is going out the door and whispers in his
ear.

'Catch me a butterfly today Abdullah,
a big green butterfly if you can.'

And Abdullah knows that Grandfather
is hungry for the porridge that he likes so
much because his teeth are all gone.

In the town, not far from Abdullah's school, is the shop of the Chinese Mr Chee.

To Abdullah, it is the most wonderful shop in all the world, with shelf upon shelf stacked full to overflowing with all manner of boxes and packets and tins.

There are rolls upon rolls of fabric to make a thousand bright sarongs, and shoes enough to fit a school full of children.

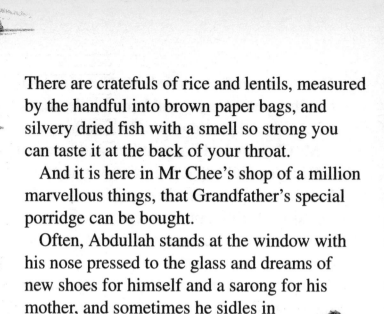

There are cratefuls of rice and lentils, measured
by the handful into brown paper bags, and
silvery dried fish with a smell so strong you
can taste it at the back of your throat.

And it is here in Mr Chee's shop of a million
marvellous things, that Grandfather's special
porridge can be bought.

Often, Abdullah stands at the window with
his nose pressed to the glass and dreams of
new shoes for himself and a sarong for his
mother, and sometimes he sidles in
through the door just to get a
smell of that wonderful fish.

Once he even dared to ask Mr Chee for a
handful, just a very small handful please,
of the special porridge for Grandfather.

Mr Chee looked down at him and frowned.
'How can it be that such a strong and
healthy boy should be begging from my shop?'
he asked. 'With arms and legs so young and
sturdy, you should easily find work to do to
earn some sen. Be off with you.'

And shamed and disappointed, Abdullah
ran out of the shop.

Chapter Six

And so it is that every day before school,
and after school when he is not working
hard at the weaving workshop, Abdullah
watches carefully for jungle creatures.

For beetles and scorpions and dragonflies,
and most especially for the jewel-winged
jungle butterflies.

Because Abdullah knows that for beetles and dragonflies and small, bright butterflies, the Craft Centre across the road from Mr Chee's shop will pay five or ten and sometimes even twenty sen, and fifty sen for a poison-tailed scorpion.

But, for a large and perfect, green-winged butterfly, he might even get one whole gold ringgit if he is lucky. Enough to buy a special treat for Grandfather. Enough to buy the porridge Grandfather likes so much, because his teeth are all gone.

The lady at the Craft Centre knows
Abdullah well, because Abdullah is very
quick and nimble with his net. Grandfather
has shown him the best places to look for
the glossy purple-backed beetles on the
forest floor.

And he is always very careful to watch
out for the bad-tempered scorpion, with its
poisonous tail curled over its back ready to
strike. Abdullah's mother is always worried
that he will be stung, but Grandfather has
shown him how to scoop them safely into
his collection box.

Even so, Abdullah's mother is glad there
aren't many scorpions to be found.

Abdullah brings lots of jungle creatures to the Craft Centre, where they are preserved and mounted on board and framed, or sometimes set in resin for key-rings and drink coasters. They are made so to be sold to the tourists as souvenirs of their visit to the highlands of Malaysia.

The lady always smiles at Abdullah when he carries in his creature box and pushes it across the bench.

'Do you have a big butterfly for me today, Abdullah?' she asks.

All too often Abdullah has to shake his head. Because the emerald-winged butterfly is a wonderful, elusive creature, and very difficult to catch.

41

Chapter Seven

On the day I was going to Abdullah's village, Abdullah rode down early to the town as usual, in the rattly old yellow school bus with the tall black writing on its side. SEKOLAH, it says. School.

'Selamat datang, Abdullah,' said the driver when Abdullah got on. 'And how is Grandfather today?'

'He is well,' said Abdullah, 'but he is
wanting some of his special porridge,
because it is hard for him to chew nuts
and pancakes and pineapples. I will have
to catch some creatures and get some
ringgit for Mr Chee.'

As the bus bumped and swerved down
the mountain, Abdullah kept watch out
of the window, twirling his net gently in
his hands, hoping to be lucky enough to
see a large, bright butterfly.

When he got off the bus at the stop near the school, Abdullah saw a dainty, darting dragonfly. He nimbly whisked it into his net, but five sen was not enough to buy Grandfather the porridge he likes so much.

Then, in the schoolyard, hunched down in
a puddle by the drinking tap he saw a small
green forest frog. Abdullah grinned with
glee. He carefully scooped it into his net
and sneaked into the classroom.

   He hung his bag on its hook, and when he
was sure no-one was looking he slipped the
frog into Siew Lian's desk and slunk out to
kick the soccer ball with his friends.

During class, Siew Lian reached into her desk to get out her writing book. Four cold sticky frog feet stepped onto her hand. She screamed and jumped out of her seat and shook the creature off, making such a fuss that everyone began to laugh. Mr Ginyun was cross.

'It is just a little frog that made its bed in your desk last night, Siew Lian,' he said. 'Sit down and do your work, and don't be such a silly.'

Abdullah smirked. Siew Lian looked around and saw and pulled a face at him.

'Poor little frog,' said Abdullah, and he reached down and picked it up from where it had hopped and stopped near his desk.

'Perhaps it is a handsome Prince needing your kiss, Siew Lian,' he teased wickedly, holding its little frog face out to her.

Siew Lian shrieked again, and ran behind Mr Ginyun's desk. 'Enough is enough,' said Mr Ginyun. 'Take the poor thing outside, now.'

When everything settled down again in class, Abdullah studied hard, as his mother told him. He studied maths and English and faraway countries.

He wrote carefully in his book and listened to Mr Ginyun, but all the while he kept one eye watching out the window for a butterfly for Grandfather.

Chapter Eight

It was on the way home from school that
Abdullah saw the butterfly. The bus pulled off
the road and stopped part-way up the mountain
to let some children off at their village.

Looking out the window, magically Abdullah
saw the butterfly resting on a leafy fern. It was
as large as a saucer and glowed green as a new
papaya leaf, hemmed with velvet black.

Not quite believing what he was seeing, he
watched it fold its wings upwards to show
the sapphire smudges underneath.

The bus started to move and Abdullah leapt out of his seat. He grabbed up his bag and butterfly net, and stumbled down the aisle.

'Wait,' he said urgently. 'Let me off.'

The driver put on the brakes, and the bus choked and jerked. Abdullah lost his balance and almost fell into the driver's lap.

'I want to get off,' Abdullah said. 'There's a butterfly back there.'

'You sure?' asked the driver. 'It's still a mighty long walk home up the mountain.'

But Abdullah nodded adamantly.
He wanted to get off, now.

He waved to his friends hanging out the windows and they waved back as the bus chugged off in a cloud of fumes and dust.

Abdullah hitched his satchel onto his back, grasped his net firmly in his hand and ran back down the road to where he had seen the butterfly.

'Let it still be there,' he whispered, with every step. 'Let it still be there.'

Like a miracle, it was still there, rocking gently on a fern frond. He held his breath in wonder and excitement, because this was the largest, most perfect butterfly of its kind he had ever seen.

It seemed to him that all the forest held its breath and waited and watched while the butterfly preened.

Abdullah stared,
almost in a trance, as,
with an upward sweep of its
brilliant wings, the butterfly launched
itself off the plant and into flight. Lofting up and
floating, floating, alighting again, then floating
up, and up . . .

So beautiful, so light and free and magnificent.
What would it be like to fly like a butterfly?
wondered Abdullah, following it with
amazement shining like stars in his eyes.

Then, remembering Grandfather, Abdullah
came to his senses. Taking a firm hold of
his bamboo net handle, he gave chase.

The emerald-winged butterfly led him
on and on and on, along the winding road,
higher up the mountain, deeper into the
rainforest. Lofting and floating, alighting
for countless seconds. Not long.
Never long . . .

Never long enough for Abdullah
to quite catch up, to quite whisk
it into his net.

Chapter Nine

Feeling hotter and hotter and tired and puffed, Abdullah chased the butterfly. He watched as the wonderful, elusive emerald creature settled itself again on the low leaf of a banana palm.

'Perhaps it too is tired and hot,' he wondered, sneaking over with his net, slowly and stealthily stalking it. And perhaps it was, because Abdullah came close. Close, closer . . . almost close enough . . . and up it lofted again, up and up . . .

No, it was not tired. Not as tired as Abdullah.
Abdullah watched it for a moment, ready
almost to give up. But he remembered
Grandfather, and he set his shoulders and
began the chase again.

He heard the motor of a car labouring up the mountain. It slowed as it went past, and he saw the lady smile and wave at him before it went around the bend.

He didn't have the strength to wave back, to even smile, and the sweat dripped into his eyes.

On and on and on the butterfly drew him. His legs were shaking and his chest was burning. He could not go much further.

Suddenly, ahead, he saw the roadside stall, and the car stopped over by the waterfall.

'Please,' he whispered. 'Please don't let the butterfly fly up into the valley of the waterfall. I cannot follow it into the thick forest there.'

He gave a grunting shout as he gathered the last of his strength and sprang after the butterfly before it was lost.

The lady stood by her car, and the butterfly fluttered on, and up, and over, and amazingly, settled on her shoulder.

'Don't move,' he whispered, knowing this was his last chance to catch it. He didn't have the strength to chase it any further.

'Don't move,' he said in a low, intense voice, never taking his eyes off the butterfly preening on her shoulder.

'Don't move,' he said, stalking closer and closer, net outstretched.

Close . . . closer . . . close enough . . .

Suddenly, the woman whirled around.

'No,' she shouted. 'You're not having it, to pin and frame and sell. I won't let you have it.'

She reached up and flicked the butterfly away.

'Shoo, shoo. Fly away butterfly, fly away free,' she said.

And the emerald-winged butterfly lifted itself once again, and floated away, above the waterfall, up into the dark, dense valley, a vivid patch of green in the leafy shadows.

Chapter Ten

Tired and hot and disappointed, Abdullah watched it go. His shoulders slumped, and defeated tears washed the dust in runnels down his cheeks.

Sensing that I was watching him, he roughly wiped his knuckles over his eyes, as though to brush away some flies.

Then he turned and stared back at me with bitter black accusing eyes.

'Why?' he asked, in a low voice. 'Why did you chase Grandfather's butterfly away?'

I asked Abdullah his name, and where he lived. He told me his village and I told him I was going there. Abdullah was excited to hear news of my friend, who had gone away from their village and away from their country, far away to further her studies. And he told me of his mother's plans for him.

On the way to the village, Abdullah told me his story. This story. About his mother and Grandfather and the weaving workshop. He showed me his butterfly net, how wondrously fine it was. And he told me about the Craft Centre and Mr Chee and the porridge that Grandfather likes so much because his teeth are all gone.

Abdullah took me into his village, and into his home, and to the home of the family of my friend. I will never forget that magical day, or Abdullah's story that told of things more magic even than jewel-winged butterflies. Things like the love of a boy for his grandfather, who once was the best weaver in all the village.

Chapter Eleven

'Did you study hard at school today?' asked
Abdullah's mother when she came home from
the weaving workshop. Because she wants him
to do more than weave baskets and catch
butterflies for the rest of his life.

'Did you catch me a butterfly today,
Abdullah?' asked Grandfather. Because he was
hoping to have some of his favourite porridge
for tea that night.

Abdullah shook his head.

'It doesn't matter,' said Grandfather.

But it did to Abdullah. He thought he would
never see another butterfly, so large and
beautiful again.

'There is always tomorrow,' said Grandfather.
'You can always catch me a
butterfly tomorrow.'

Then Abdullah remembered.
He remembered the frog, and he made Grandfather laugh with the story.

And he remembered the dragonfly on the way to school. He went and got it out of the creature box. Its wings shone like spun silver in the evening light.

If he could catch another dragonfly tomorrow, and perhaps a scorpion, and a beetle or two . . . there would be enough to buy Grandfather the porridge he likes so much.

But not today. There was not time enough
left today.

Tomorrow.

The Sea-Baby

AND OTHER MAGICAL STORIES TO READ ALOUD

Compiled by Susan Dickinson
Illustrated by Peter Bailey

The moon was bright and filled the square of my window pane with silver light; and through the air outside I saw something swimming – I thought at first it was a white cloud, but as it reached my open window I saw it was a lady, moving along the air as though she were swimming in water.

Eleven magical stories featuring ghosts and witches; babies and pixies; a magic glove and a magic horse, as well as cats, a starry cloak and three silver balls in a collection that ranges from much-loved traditional stories to new stories from some of today's finest writers for children.

Enchanting, funny and fantastical – these stories are perfect for reading aloud to young children or for older children to read, enjoy and clamour for more!

A GOOSEY FARM STORY

A DOG'S JOURNEY
Gene Kemp

"The summer we went to live at Goosey was
magic – the sun seemed to shine all day long."

For the first time in their lives, Widget and her
little brother Tim can roam about the hills and
fields with their two dogs Russet and Dizzy
Frizzy. And Sam the Boss Cat is never far
away, usually waiting to pounce on Russet!
After a shaky start – and a few scraps – Tim and
Widget are making new friends. With the
added excitement of puppies to look forward
to, everything seems perfect at Goosey. But
autumn brings change and, with the first
sparkle of frost in the air, comes an
unforgettable tragedy...

*A heart-warming story from one of today's best-
loved authors. Carnegie medallist Gene Kemp's
exquisite writing brings a breath of country air
to all young readers.*

SPIDER McDREW
by Alan Durant

Spider McDrew is a hopeless case.
Everybody says so. He's so busy
dreaming he's often one step behind
everyone else. But he does have a
special talent for surprises. Whether
playing football or performing in
the school play, Spider *always* has a
surprise in store.

Order Form

To order direct from the publishers, just make a list of the titles you want and fill in the form below:

Name ....

Address ....

....

....

Send to: Dept 6, HarperCollins Publishers Ltd, Westerhill Road, Bishopbriggs, Glasgow G64 2QT.

Please enclose a cheque or postal order to the value of the cover price, plus:

UK & BFPO: Add £1.00 for the first book, and 25p per copy for each additional book ordered.

Overseas and Eire: Add £2.95 service charge. Books will be sent by surface mail but quotes for airmail despatch will be given on request.

A 24-hour telephone ordering service is available to holders of Visa, MasterCard, Amex or Switch cards on 0141- 772 2281.

Collins
An *Imprint* of HarperCollins*Publishers*